THE
MAGIC
CHEST

Dancing Til' Dusk

D.G. THOMAS

DEDICATION

For Jesse

ACKNOWLEDGEMENTS

Illustrated by
Sudipta Basu

Published in the United States of America by
Mattison Savage Publishing
Louisville, KY
www.authordgthomas.com

Check out the end of the book to get a FREE gift from the author!

───────── ● ─────────

Don't miss book #3

The Magic Chest

Halloween Hideout

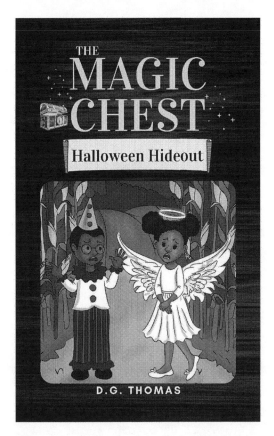

Read all of the books in the series to follow the entire adventure! **_If you enjoyed this book, kindly leave a review online wherever books are sold._**

Learn more about the series at:
authordgthomas.com

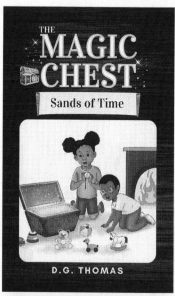

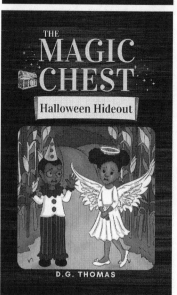

CONTENTS

PROLOGUE

The Magic Chest book series explores the adventures of seven-year-old Ethan and his nine-year-old sister Jessie. The children move from New Jersey to John's Island, South Carolina with their parents into a 100-year-old farmhouse they inherited from their grandfather who recently passed away.

Jessie and Ethan find a magical wooden chest inside the attic of the old house. There are four items in the chest that take the children back in time on an adventure where they meet special friends and learn the mystery behind each item. In book one, *Sands of Time*, Ethan and Jessie met Sam and learned about the gold pocket watch.

There are three remaining items in the chest.

CHAPTER ONE
A Hot Afternoon

It was a hot, sticky, humid Saturday afternoon on John's Island. Ethan happily played outside on the old tire swing tied to an oak tree. Sweat rolled off Jessie's face as she tried to keep cool by gulping down her ice-cold lemonade. Mom and Dad were swinging back and forth on the wooden porch swing while sipping their lemonade.

"What a beautiful day," Mom said as she stretched her arms out to relax.

"Yep, it sure is," Dad agreed with Mom as they looked at each other and smiled.

"It's so hot out here!" Ethan yelled.

"Yeah, can we go in the house now and watch TV or something?" Jessie pleaded.

"When you grow up and work as hard as we do you'll appreciate sunny days and lemonade," Dad said as he got up and went inside the house.

Suddenly, the loud sound of music, jazz music, with trumpets and saxophones started playing and blasted loudly out of the windows of the old farmhouse. Dad put an old fifties jazz record on the record player and it was as if the house had come alive.

He stepped back outside onto the front porch, reached his hand out to Mom who was still swinging, and asked, "May I have this dance, my lady?"

"Why, yes you can sir," Mom answered in her best Southern accent.

Mom and Dad laughed as they danced on the front porch. Jessie and Ethan even twirled in circles in the front yard to the music for a few minutes until they both fell down on the ground and burst into laughter.

14

"Hey Jessie, we should go look inside the magic chest again," Ethan said.

"I don't know. I didn't think we were going to make it back home last time," Jessie said.

"But we did make it back, so come on let's go!" Ethan ranted as he eagerly ran upstairs.

"Wait for me!" Jessie said.

"Mom, Dad, we're going to the attic to play," Jessie said to her parents as she ran upstairs behind Ethan.

"What did Jessie say?" asked Mom.

"I don't know, something about playing. Let's just keep dancing dear," said Dad.

"Well, okay dear," she replied.

Then they continued to dance to the lively jazz music.

CHAPTER TWO

The Sound of Music

Once inside the attic the children wasted no time opening the magic chest. They looked at each other excited about the other items in the chest and where they might go. Jessie took a deep breath, and Ethan reached inside the chest and pulled out a brass trumpet.

"Cool, I bet this belonged to Sam," Ethan said. He put the old trumpet to his lips and blew air inside.

Dom! Dom! Dom!

A loud flat noise came out of the trumpet

and the children giggled. Suddenly, a note on old parchment paper appeared to be floating above the chest from out of nowhere. Jessie grabbed the note and read it aloud. The note said:

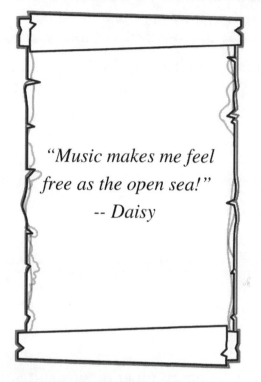

"Music makes me feel free as the open sea!"
-- Daisy

"Who is Daisy?" Jessie asked.

"I don't know, but this trumpet is awesome!" Ethan exclaimed and he continued to terribly play the old trumpet.

"Ethan, I know I can't read music, but those look like music notes coming out of the trumpet?"

"Whoa!" Ethan said as he stopped blowing the trumpet and looked up around the room. The sound of music began to fill the attic, but Ethan was no longer playing the trumpet. The music seemed to come from nowhere, but as the children listened closer they could tell the music was coming from the trumpet. The sound of a piano, flutes, trumpets, and drums playing a beautiful song followed by music notes all came from the trumpet.

"Jessie, the music is coming from the trumpet!" he shouted.

"How is that happening?" Jessie asked.

"It's magic!" Ethan said with delight as he laughed and twirled in circles.

Ethan held the trumpet in his hand and the sound of music filled the air and encircled the children. Their ears overflowed with the soft beautiful melody of classical music and they smiled and danced in the attic. They were amazed as they looked at the music notes dancing in the air.

Suddenly, the attic window flew open. A strong gust of wind ripped its way into the attic creating a spiraling funnel of sparkling white sand. The children stood still and watched in amazement as the sands of time began to swirl and form a circle around them until they were completely surrounded.

"It's happening again!" Jessie yelled.

"*Woo, hoo... uh, oh,* I can't move!" Ethan shouted.

"I can't move either!" Jessie tried to yell over the loud music.

The children felt as though they were swirling inside of an hourglass and free falling unable to stop the sands of time from taking them away.

Ethan struggled to get closer to his sister.

"Jessie, the sand is taking me away!"

"Me too!" she shouted.

21

Ethan and Jessie were overcome with the sand, the sight of music notes, bright lights, stars, and the sound of music until they could no longer see or hear anything else around them.

Then they let out a loud scream.

Suddenly, everything stopped. The attic was empty, peacefully quiet, and the children were gone.

CHAPTER THREE
Dress Rehearsal

The wind stopped. The sparkling white sand and the circle of musical notes fell to the ground and disappeared. Then the loud classical music slowly fell silent from the children's ears.

They opened their eyes and they were standing in the middle of a stage. It was a practice dress rehearsal for a musical show the room was filled with children. Some were playing instruments and some were dancing. No one seemed to notice that Ethan and Jessie just appeared in the room out of nowhere.

A man wearing a black suit and top hat pointed directly at Jessie and Ethan. "You two standing over there, go get in position!"

"Where do we need to go?" Ethan asked.

"You're holding drumsticks and you're wearing a leotard, tutu, and ballet slippers. Please tell me you haven't forgotten the song or dance routine too! Now go to your sections *PLEASE* we don't have any time to waste!" he yelled.

They looked around and saw a group of ballerinas and orchestra performers. Ethan, dressed in a small black tuxedo, nervously ran to the drum section in the orchestra.

While Jessie, dressed in a soft pink leotard, tutu, and pink satin ballet slippers ran to the section with the other dancers.

"*Ouch, Ouch,*" Jessie mumbled as she ran across the floor in the tight satin ballet slippers that hurt her feet.

"Ok, everyone get into your places," said Miss Sarah, a beautiful dance teacher wearing a red dress and black high heeled shoes.

All the dancers stood in their positions on the floor, holding their arms loose to their sides and turning their feet to a 90-degree angle. Jessie found an empty spot on the stage floor and did her best to stand just like the other dancers.

Then the music in the orchestra began to play and Miss Sarah was holding a straight cane, and tapping it on the floor while she counted. "1, 2, 3...1, 2, 3...

"Sallie lift your arm higher, more graceful, like a beautiful swan. Terry, twirl her with more power," Miss Sarah instructed.

Jessie noticed that Miss Sarah gave out command after command to all the dancers. Especially to the two dancers in front of everyone else on stage. The young dancers were very tired but never stopped dancing.

All the other dancers began twirling around in circles. They looked like pink flower petals blowing in the wind as they twirled and danced.

Jessie felt her legs move and somehow she knew the dance steps!

26

She began twirling and gliding around the stage, like a graceful swan. Her movements were perfect. She didn't know how she was able to dance, but she thought dancing to the orchestra's music was fun.

The man in the black top hat's name was Mr. Dunbar. He was the orchestra music conductor. Ethan was playing with the other members of the orchestra.

Mr. Dunbar lifted a stick that looked like a wand, then he began to count, and everyone began to play their instruments. First, a girl on piano, followed by the trumpet section, flute section, and other wind instruments. Then the chimes and finally he pointed to the drums.

Ethan's hands lifted the drumsticks to play the drum set in front of him with the orchestra and somehow he knew the song and how to play the drums! He played the drum beat perfectly along with the other musical instruments.

When the practice was over everyone complimented each other on the work they did for the rehearsal as they began packing their things to go home.

"Everyone, get plenty of rest. The show will start tonight at 5:00 pm. Let's make this the best musical performance Harlem has seen in 1953!" announced Mr. Dunbar.

"*Yay! Yay!*" all of the young dancers and musicians cheered and clapped their hands as they left the rehearsal hall.

Jessie looked at Ethan across the room and silently mouthed the words "Harlem 1953!" Then she walked over to Ethan. "We have to find the brass trumpet."

"Do you think it will help us get back home?" he asked.

Jessie rubbed her toes. "It has to get us home or we'll be stuck here in 1953 forever. I don't want to be stuck here. My feet hurt in these shoes!"

"Ok, let's split up and see if we can figure out who has it," Ethan suggested.

"Good idea!" Jessie agreed.

Then a group of ballerinas pulled Jessie backstage with them to talk about the show.

Meanwhile, Ethan went to talk with some kids in the orchestra to find the brass trumpet.

CHAPTER FOUR
Daisy

"Hey, you're really good at playing those drums, think you could show me how to play sometime?" asked a little girl standing behind Ethan.

Ethan turned around slowly and saw a little girl with two long pigtail braids in her hair. She was wearing a black and white tuxedo, a top hat and holding a trumpet.

The trumpet from the magic chest!

"Who me, um sure, I can teach you to play the drums.

If you show me how to play that trumpet," Ethan replied.

The little girl didn't know that Ethan didn't really know how to play the drums, and he didn't want her to find out.

"Wow, you bet! Can you show me some moves this afternoon before tonight's show? I've got a drum set at my house," the girl asked.

"Sure thing, I have to bring my sister. Is that okay? She's a dancer," Ethan said.

The girl was so excited about learning to play drums. "Yep, she can come too."

"Wait here and I'll go get her," Ethan said.

Ethan ran over to Jessie who was talking to some of the other dancers.

Ethan whispered into Jessie's ear as he pointed over to the little girl, then waved and smiled at her. "I found the trumpet from the magic chest. That little girl over there has it."

"Are you sure it's the same one?" Jessie asked.

"Yep, and she invited us over to her house, so I can teach her some of my drum moves!" Ethan said proudly.

"Ethan, you don't really have any drum moves!"

"Shhh! don't say that too loud someone might hear you," Ethan said.

"Besides, that girl doesn't know that I can't really play drums. She doesn't know how to play either so what difference does it make?" Ethan said with a smile on his face.

"Oh brother!" Jessie said as she scratched her head.

"Come on, she's waiting on us," Ethan said as he took his sister by the arm and dragged her across the room with her feet being pinched by the tight ballet slippers all of the way across the stage.

"Hi, I'm Jessie. I see you've met my brother Ethan."

"I can't wait to learn those smooth moves Ethan has with the drums," the girl said.

"Yeah, that's me Mr. Smooth!" Ethan bragged while rubbing his chin.

Jessie nudged Ethan on his shoulder.

"Hey, what was that for?" Ethan said.

"Come on guys let's go. My mom is here to pick me up. Have you asked your mom if you can go home with me yet?" the little girl asked.

"Our mom won't mind. Hey why are you dressed in a tuxedo and playing in the orchestra? Don't you like dancing?" Jessie asked.

"I used to dance, but I don't anymore. It's a long story. I really don't want to talk about it," the girl said.

"I'm glad you can come home with me today! By the way my name is Daisy Brown."

"*Daisy?*" Ethan and Jessie whispered quietly together as they looked at each other puzzled.

CHAPTER FIVE
Unexpected Guests

Jessie and Ethan followed Daisy outside. They got inside the car with Daisy and her mom and traveled home with their new friend.

"Is it okay with your parents for you to come over and play?" Daisy's mom asked.

"How did you know we had parents?" asked Ethan who was a little confused.

"What?" asked Daisy's mom.

"Umm....what my brother means is that my parents had to leave town quickly, and we don't have anywhere to stay tonight after the show.

Can we spend the night with Daisy and you?" Jessie asked quickly hoping she would not get suspicious.

"Oh, you poor dears! I have to ask Daisy's dad, but I don't think that should be a problem," Daisy's Mom said.

Daisy was an only child and her parents thought it was nice for the two children to come over and play with her. Daisy's mom thought that she had been kind of sad ever since Daisy and her best friend Sallie had stopped talking. They pulled up into the driveway of a large home just outside of the city.

"Man, this is a lot bigger than Sam's house," Ethan whispered to Jessie.

"and our house," Jessie replied.

The children got out of the car and went inside the house. It had shiny white marble floors, a crystal chandelier hanging from the ceiling and a spiral staircase that lead to the rooms upstairs.

"Whoa!" the children said together at the same time.

"Are you rich or something?" Ethan asked curiously.

"Ethan!" Jessie shouted as she nudged her brother. She was embarrassed, but also wanted to know if Daisy was rich too.

"May I take your coat and hat sir?" a man dressed in a suit asked as he reached his hand out to take Ethan's coat and hat.

Ethan giggled and said to the man "my name's not sir. It's Ethan. Yes, you can have my coat and hat, but I think it's too small for you," Ethan replied.

Jessie looked at Daisy. "Is that your Dad?"

"Yes, that's my Dad. His name is Bentley. He's also the Butler around here."

"I knew you were rich, only rich people have a butler!" Ethan exclaimed.

"We're not rich, but we are blessed. We work for and live with the Calhoun family. Mr. Calhoun is very wealthy and owns several businesses in Harlem. They're really nice people and treat my husband, Daisy, and myself like family," Daisy's mom explained.

"My mom says we're blessed too, but we don't have nothin' like this house!" Jessie said.

Everyone laughed and Daisy's mom told the children to go upstairs to her room to play while she went to prepare lunch for everyone.

"My mom is the cook here and she is the best cook ever!" said Daisy.

"Oh, by the way, children would you like me to prepare chicken, duck, or a rack of lamb for lunch?" Daisy's mom asked.

"Are you serious?" Jessie asked.

"I'll take the rack of lamb please," Ethan said in a fake English accent.

"Ethan, you don't even know what lamb tastes like!" Jessie said.

"Mom, can we just get cheeseburgers and fries," Daisy said.

"Yes, that sounds delicious," Jessie said.

"Hmm, well if you insist on eating such a common meal!" Ethan said in his fake English accent as he playfully turned up his nose and walked away.

The children entered Daisy's room that was small and tidy with a few toys and her drum set.

"Man it looks like a flamingo threw up in here!" Ethan said.

The color pink was on everything in the room. The walls, floor, bed and even the drum set.

"Sorry Ethan, I know a lot of boys don't usually like pink, but it's my favorite color," Daisy said.

"It's ok, hey let's start practicing and begin with the trumpet?" Ethan said.

Daisy began to play the trumpet. A beautiful melody came from the brass instrument so clear and easy. As Daisy played the trumpet, Ethan and Jessie began laughing, twirling around in circles and dancing to the music.

"Wow! You are great playing the trumpet!" said Jessie.

"Yep, now it's my turn. Be still and watch the master do his work!" Ethan boasted.

The boy picked up the trumpet and began blowing.

Dom! Dink! Dom! Dom! Dink! Dom! Dow!

Horrible loud noises that were off-key came from the instrument as Daisy and Jessie put their fingers in their ears to make the noise quieter. They closed their eyes and cringed as the noise Ethan played became more and more painful to hear.

The girls both laughed then Daisy said "Okay, I think it's my turn to learn drums now."

"Well, what did you think?" Ethan asked.

"Umm, well, I think you need a little more practice," Daisy said with a smile.

"Don't worry you'll pick up in no time. Come on show me those drum moves of yours," Daisy said.

Ethan sat down in front of the drum set, stretched his arms, cracked his knuckles then picked up the drumsticks and began banging on the drums over and over. Once again Ethan played off beat.

Bang! Bang! Bang! Bang!
Bang! Bang! Bang! Bang!

Ethan played the drums just as bad as he played the trumpet.

43

"Wait a minute I thought you could play the drums. You sounded so good back at the theatre," Daisy said.

"I don't know what's happening. Maybe there was something magical at the theatre?" Ethan slyly suggested.

"Oh no, I was really hoping to learn how to play the drums from you. I'm really tired of playing the trumpet!" Daisy said.

"Why? You're so good at it," Jessie said.

"I only started playing the trumpet, because I love music so much and wanted to stay in the show. I used to be a dancer and I loved dancing most but, I quit when my former best friend Sallie and her friends Norma and Betty started bullying me," Daisy explained.

Just then the front door opened, then slammed shut. "What's that noise?" Ethan asked as he and Jessie peeped over the railing at the top of the staircase to see who had come inside of the house.

"Please come back," Daisy fearfully pled with Ethan and Jessie to come to back to her room.

"What's wrong?" Jessie asked.

Then she heard a child's voice and looked over the railing again.

"Isn't that the girl from recital practice?" Jessie asked.

"Yep, that's her," said Ethan loudly as he looked over the railing, "and she's real bossy!" he said.

"Bentley, take our things!" demanded the little girl as she and her two friends rudely tossed their dance tote bags at the butler.

"Miss Jeanie what's for lunch?" the little girl asked Daisy's mom.

"Cheeseburgers and french fries" Daisy's mom replied.

"Ugh! Cheeseburgers and french fries! Are you kidding? I'm a prima ballerina. I can't possibly dance tonight and eat a cheeseburger and fries! Just fix three salads. One salad for me and a salad for each of my friends!" demanded the bossy little ballerina.

She and her two friends stomped up the stairs and into the room across the hall from Daisy.

Daisy was able to pull Jessie and Ethan back into her room just before the girls got to the top of the stairs.

"Who was that?" Ethan asked curiously.

"That was Sallie Calhoun. My former best friend," Daisy said.

"What is she doing here? Does she live with you?" Jessie asked.

"No. My family works for Sallie's family. I live with her."

CHAPTER SIX
Sallie

Sallie Calhoun, Mr. Calhoun's daughter, grew up with Daisy, and the two girls were like sisters.

"We always played together but, things changed when we joined dance class. Miss Sarah, our teacher, thought that I was a better dancer than Sallie and the other girls in the class.

She put me in the lead role for the show, and Sallie got really mad," Daisy explained.

"If you two were close like sisters why wasn't she happy for you?" Jessie asked.

"She got really jealous that she had to be my understudy and she said since her father was paying for the classes that I should be her understudy," Daisy said.

"After that day, Sallie and her friends, Norma and Betty, started calling me names. They dance too and didn't like me being in the lead role either. Sallie told everyone I was poor and worked as a maid for her family. She told everyone we were never really friends," Daisy said.

"That was really mean. What did you do?" Ethan asked.

"Everyone laughed at me. I was so embarrassed and it really hurt my feelings, so I quit the show. Then I missed the music and everyone else so much I decided to join the orchestra.

That way I could still be in the show and stay far away from Sallie at least while I was there. We both still live together here and she always gives me mean looks."

"That's just terrible, but at least you didn't completely quit the show," Jessie said as she tried to help Daisy feel better.

"After I quit the show Sallie took my place as the lead dancer because she was my understudy," Daisy said.

"What's an understudy?" Ethan asked.

"It's the person who studies the dance moves at the same time as the lead dancer. Just in case something happens to the lead dancer the show can still go on because someone else knows what to do," Daisy explained.

"You know what the worst part is? Later on, I found out that Sallie, Norma, and Betty had planned to get me to quit the show all along so that Sallie could dance in the lead role," said Daisy.

Daisy lowered her head and looked sad. "Now I'm stuck playing the trumpet. I thought I could switch to the drums. That's why I wanted Ethan to help me, but seeing Jessie in her pretty pink tutu only reminds me of how much I really miss dancing."

CHAPTER SEVEN
Before the Show

"Sallie, you're the best dancer ever!" Norma exclaimed.

"Miss Sarah never should've given your maid, I mean Daisy the lead role. She's nowhere near as good of a dancer as you are," said Betty.

"You're right girls, and tonight when I star in the show everyone will know I'm the best dancer here, and since we got Miss Pig Tail braids out of her ballet slippers I never have to worry about losing a dance lead to her ever again," bragged Sallie.

Then the three girls laughed together about getting Daisy out of the lead dancing role.

Daisy was standing on the outside of Sallie's dressing room door and had overheard the girls talking about her. She became angry and stormed into the dressing room, Jessie followed her, while Ethan waited outside the door.

"Sallie, you and I were best friends why would you treat me like this?" said Daisy.

"I would never be best friends with my maid," Sallie replied as she laughed and turned her nose up in the air at Daisy.

Daisy pointed her finger at Sallie. "I don't want to be friends with you anymore. You have been so mean to me. You knew how much dancing meant to me and you didn't care how bad this would hurt my feelings. You are not better than me just because your family has more money than my family!"

Sallie folded her arms across her chest and looked the other way as if she didn't care, but secretly she felt bad that she had hurt her friend. She rolled her eyes, turned away from Daisy and marched out of the dressing room. Norma and Betty followed her.

"Man she really told you!" Ethan said with a smile on his face as the three ballerinas walked past him.

"*Humph!*" Sallie mumbled under her breath.

She rolled her eyes and stomped her feet as she walked past Ethan onto the stage to get ready to dance for the show.

Jessie reached out and gave Daisy a hug. "Wow, I'm proud of you for standing up for yourself!"

"Come on Daisy, we've got to get to the orchestra for one last practice before the show," Ethan said.

He heard the conductor's final call for everyone to come to the stage. Ethan, Daisy and Jessie ran to the stage to take their places along with the bad attitude ballerinas.

CHAPTER EIGHT
Break a Leg

"Places everyone," said Miss Sarah.

Miss Sarah instructed the dancers to move into position. "Sallie and Terry need to be front and center," she said.

The orchestra began playing the beautiful classical music and Sallie gracefully did her dance moves with Terry. Terry moved off stage and Sallie began a dance act with Norma and Betty.

Then for the grand finale Sallie took one last solo leap into the air. When she landed back onto the floor, she accidently fell on her ankle instead of her foot and fell down on the stage!

Everyone heard a loud noise that sounded like .....*"Snap!"*

Sallie had broken her leg!

The music stopped and everyone was in shock looking at Sallie lying on the floor, holding her broken leg and crying.

"Oh no, I can't believe that happened! This is terrible," Norma said.

"Yeah, this is terrible. Hey, I wonder if Miss Sarah will let me dance in the lead role now?" asked Betty.

"You! If anyone should dance the lead it should be me! After all I'm a better dancer than you!" Norma argued.

Betty snapped back at Norma. "Oh, no you're not! You dance like a duck with two left feet!"

"Well, if I dance like a duck you dance like a chicken!" Norma yelled back at Betty.

The two ballerinas were so busy arguing over which one of them should dance the lead in the show, they forgot that Sallie was still on the floor moaning in pain!

"Norma! Betty! I thought you two were my friends! How could you fight over who's going to take my place? I need both of you to help me!" Sallie screamed and continued to cry in pain.

Norma looked down at Sallie then rolled her eyes and looked away. "Help you? I'm not a doctor. I don't know what to do," she said.

Betty shrugged her shoulders and agreed. "Me either."

Then Norma and Betty continued to argue and insult each other fighting over who would take Sallie's place in the show, while Sallie laid on the stage floor by herself crying.

Meanwhile, Miss Sarah was busy calling the ambulance and Mr. Dunbar was trying to keep everyone else calm, but no one thought to go sit with Sallie.

"Come on, let's go help her," said Daisy.

"What! Why do you want to help her?" asked Ethan.

"I thought you weren't her friend anymore," said Jessie.

"Just letting her lay there crying all by herself is mean. I don't want to be mean like her. Maybe if I treat her the way I want to be treated she can learn the right way to be a friend," Daisy said.

Then Daisy, Ethan and Jessie went and sat by Sallie's side. While all of the other ballerinas argued and fought with each other about who would take Sallie's leading role in the show.

"Why are you being so nice to me?" Sallie asked.

"I'm sorry this happened to you," said Daisy.

"I'm sorry I was mean to you and treated you so bad," said Sallie.

"I forgive you for how you treated me," said Daisy.

"Daisy, do you think we can be friends again?" asked Sallie.

"You bet!" she replied then leaned over and gave Sallie a hug.

Jessie, Ethan, and Daisy waited with Sallie until the emergency workers came by ambulance and took her away to the hospital.

CHAPTER NINE

The Show Must Go On

"Okay, everyone settle down!" shouted Miss Sarah, the dance teacher, as she urged everyone to be quiet.

"Listen everyone, the show is starting in less than an hour. We have to replace Sallie in the show and I only know of one dancer here that knows Sallie's part."

Miss Sarah looked around the crowded room filled with dancers and musicians. "Daisy, where are you?"

Everyone began to whisper.

Daisy nervously stepped from behind Jessie and Ethan and to the front of the room wearing her tuxedo, top hat and carrying her trumpet.

"Yes, Miss Sarah."

Miss Sarah looked at Daisy and smiled. "Daisy, you have always been such a graceful dancer. You bend and lean gently like a flower blown by a soft breeze. I don't know why you quit dancing, but Daisy the dancing flower, please lead our show tonight."

Daisy looked around the room and everyone, except Norma and Betty, were smiling and nodding their heads in agreement with Miss Sarah.

Daisy still felt a little unsure of herself after everything that had happened with her friend. "But...what if I mess up?"

Jessie shouted across the room. "You can do it Daisy!"

"Yeah, we believe in you!" Ethan agreed.

Soon everyone in the room began to clap and cheer on Daisy except Norma and Betty.

"Humph! I can't believe this!" said Betty.

"Yeah, me either I'm outta here, come on Betty!" Norma agreed.

The two bad attitude ballerinas stomped their feet as they marched off stage.

"See ya, wouldn't want to be ya!" Ethan shouted as the two girls marched past him.

Jessie reached out to her brother and gave him a high five. "You got that right, bro!"

Miss Sarah looked at Daisy. "Now, you just need to believe in yourself...and change your clothes of course."

"Okay, I'll do it!"

Daisy was nervous, but excited to dance again. Then she went backstage to find a leotard, tutu, tights, and ballet slippers to change into for the show.

CHAPTER TEN
Bravo!

"Places everyone, it's time for the show to start," Miss Sarah announced.

The musicians ran to the orchestra. The dancers all assumed their positions on stage behind the closed dark red velvet curtain. The lights were dim and Jessie could hear the people in the audience whispering on the other side of the curtain as they waited for the show to begin. She felt her heart pounding hard and fast in her chest as she waited for the curtain to rise.

Ethan was also eager for the show to start. He kept rocking back and forth anxious to get started.

Mr. Dunbar pointed at Ethan and whispered. "Be still. The show is about to start."

"Sorry!" Ethan shouted back loudly and everyone in the orchestra looked at him and whispered *"Shh!"* Ethan just shrugged his shoulders and smiled.

Mr. Dunbar lifted his wand and the orchestra began to play the soft melody of beautiful classical music. First, the piano, next the wind instruments, followed by the strings, drums and finally chimes.

The red velvet curtain opened and everyone in the audience could see the dancers already standing in their positions on stage ready to dance. The bright stage lights beamed down onto the stage that was decorated like a spring garden with colorful flowers and a sparkling glitter rainbow. The dancers, dressed in pink leotards and tutus, gracefully twirled across the stage dancing to the music.

Jessie was twirling around the stage and leaping through the air as if she had been dancing for years like the other ballerinas.

"I don't know what's happening, but I hope it doesn't stop," she thought.

Ethan couldn't believe how perfect he was playing the drums. It was like he had robotic arms. *"Wow! I really sound like I know what I'm doing!"* he thought.

The ballerinas parted on the stage. Half of the dancers went to the left and the other half went to the right side of the stage.

Suddenly, Daisy twirled onto the stage dressed in a white leotard and tutu covered in silver sequins that sparkled under the bright stage lights.

She was graceful and danced her routine with Terry perfectly.

In the grand finale, Daisy leaped through the air across the stage so high that she looked like a bird soaring through the sky. She landed softly on her feet then perfectly posed into Terry's arms.

The crowd jumped to their feet and roared with excitement applauding. Daisy stood on her toes in the center of the stage, with a big smile on her face and took a bow as everyone cheered and shouted *"Bravo! Bravo!"*

CHAPTER ELEVEN

After the Show

After the show, Miss Sarah was very excited and made an announcement to the dancers and musicians backstage. "I am so proud of everyone here tonight for doing such a fabulous job! Now for the best part let's go downstairs and celebrate!"

Everyone cheered, laughed, talked, and happily went downstairs to the after party. The party room that was decorated with red and white balloons and streamers. The tables were covered with white tablecloths and red confetti was sprinkled on top of each table.

The band played Doo-wop songs and there was a buffet of food to eat and fruit punch to drink. Everyone began dancing on the dance floor to celebrate.

Jessie looked around the party room. "Wow! It looks awesome in here!"

Ethan already had grabbed a plate of meatballs that he was shoving into his mouth.

"Everything tastes awesome too!" he exclaimed as he washed the meatballs down with a big gulp of fruit punch.

"Come on you guys let's dance!" said Daisy still wearing her tutu and her top hat. She began playing her trumpet with the band and dancing.

After dancing for several songs Jessie, Ethan and Daisy sat down.

"I wish I could dance and play the trumpet like you Daisy," said Jessie.

"I wish I could play the trumpet like you too and it was pretty cool the way you stood up to Sallie!" said Ethan.

"Thanks, guys. Just keep practicing and you'll get better. I'm glad I met both of you and that we are all friends," she said.

"Oh, I love this song the band is playing. Music makes me feel free as the open sea!" exclaimed Daisy as she listened to the music.

"I could dance until dusk," she said.

"Dusk, what's that?" asked Ethan.

"Just until the sun goes down, so I better hurry up I don't have much time left," Daisy said as she laughed, ran back out onto the dance floor, and kept dancing to the Doo-wop music.

"Ethan, do you hear that? Why is the band playing louder?" Jessie yelled.

"The music does sound like it's getting louder," Ethan noticed.

"Wait. Daisy just said the magic words," said Jessie.

"What magic words?" Ethan asked.

"The words on the paper in the magic chest. I think that's what takes us home. Look around, it's happening again," said Jessie.

Jessie and Ethan looked around and everyone at the party was frozen in time including Daisy.

Suddenly, a strong gust of wind rushed through a window into the party room. Instead of the Doo-wop music from the party, they began to hear the same music from the attic. The sound grew louder and louder.

Then they saw the musical notes, bright lights, stars, and the sparkling white sands of time. The sand began to circle and swirl around the children until they could only see each other in the calm center of the funnel of sand.

"I can't move," said Jessie.

"I'm stuck too," said Ethan.

Then the children felt as though they were free falling. Swirling faster and faster down through the sand as if they were in an hourglass.

Overcome with the sand, the sight of music notes, bright lights, stars, and the sound of music, the children could no longer see or hear anything else around them.

In a flash of light, Ethan and Jessie disappeared from the party.

CHAPTER TWELVE
Grandma

A bright light flashed, all of the sparkling white sand fell to the ground then disappeared. The children found themselves back in the attic, on the floor, kneeling in front of the open chest. Ethan still had the brass trumpet in his hand.

"Ethan, that's Daisy's trumpet!"

"How did we get back in the attic?" Ethan asked.

"The sand. The sand is how we travel through time," Jessie said.

The children heard their mother's voice call them. "Ethan. Jessie. It's time for family game night. Come downstairs."

Although the children felt as though they had been gone for an entire day, no time seemed to have passed at their home. Mom and Dad had just finished dancing and were taking out board games and popping popcorn for family game night.

"Look, I found some of grandma's old records. Did you know that Grandma was a really good dancer and played the trombone or maybe it was the trumpet professionally? Anyway, here is one of the songs she recorded," said Mom. Then she handed an old album cover over to Jessie.

Jessie admired the picture of the beautiful older lady on the cover. She had golden brown skin, thick curly sandy brown hair, and was holding a trumpet. Jessie thought something about her face looked familiar. "Grandma was really beautiful!" she said.

While she was admiring the picture on the album cover something fell out of it. Jessie reached down to the floor to pick it up.

"Look, Ethan!" Jessie exclaimed. It was a picture of Daisy in her tuxedo holding a trumpet.

"Mom, where did you get this picture of Daisy?" Jessie asked.

"Daisy? Since when have you been on a first-name basis with your grandmother?" she asked.

I think she was about eight years old when this picture was taken. She always said it was from some big stage show she did in the 50's that changed her life," Mom said as she handed the picture to Ethan.

"So she stopped dancing?" Ethan asked.

"I don't remember telling you that your Grandma used to dance. She said after the big stage show she decided she loved dancing but loved playing the trumpet more, so she decided to be a musician. She went on to play in a band and record albums like this one," Mom said.

"Wow! That's amazing," said Jessie and Ethan.

Ethan whispered to Jessie. "I can't believe Daisy's our Grandmother."

"I think it's awesome!" Jessie exclaimed.

"I do too," said Ethan.

Dad put one of Grandma's old Doo-wop records on the record player and Ethan and Jessie began to dance and spin around the room in circles laughing.

"What's gotten into those two?" Dad asked.

"Who knows, but maybe we should dance too!" Mom said as she reached out and took Dad's hand and began dancing.

After spinning in circles Ethan and Jessie fell onto the floor. Ethan put his arms under his head and looked up at the ceiling.

"I wonder where the magic chest will take us next time?" Ethan asked.

Jessie smiled and said, "I don't know. I guess we'll just have to take another look inside."

About the Author

D.G.Thomas' first book *The Magic Chest: Sands of Time* grew out of a love for telling bedtime stories to her children. Since then the author has written and published three other books in *The Magic Chest Book Series: Dancing Til' Dusk, Halloween Hideout, and Seaside Treasure.* She also wrote *Flower Power Unicorns, Norris and Twig,* and other picture books. Thomas is a graduate of the University of Louisville and a member of the Society of Children's Book Writer's and Illustrators. She resides in Kentucky, where the grass isn't really blue, with her daughter, son, and their curious cat.

Learn more about D.G. Thomas' books and follow her on social media for the latest updates:

Author website: www.authordgthomas.com

Facebook: @AuthorDGThomas

Twitter: @dg_thomas

Instagram: @authordgthomas

Thank you for purchasing this book!
As a special thank you please
download the FREE activity coloring
and puzzle pages for The Magic
Chest: Sands of Time. Enjoy!

Download here:
https://bit.ly/magicchestfree

or

SCAN ME

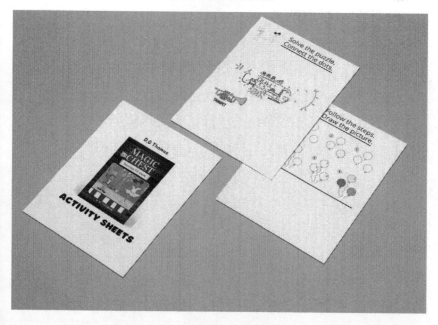

Dear Reader,

Thank you for reading *The Magic Chest: Dancing Til' Dusk*. I hope you liked it. If you enjoyed the book, I'd be grateful if you share a short review online wherever books are sold. Your feedback really makes a difference and helps others learn about my books. I appreciate your support!

Visit my website to learn more fun facts about The Magic Chest Book Series, download FREE fun activity and coloring pages, and learn about my new books (Sometimes I give away FREE copies!) visit **www.authordgthomas.com.**

Thank you!
DG Thomas

Made in the USA
Columbia, SC
13 March 2024

32704178R00052